THE SHADOW OF MATILDA HUNT

Deborah Zemke

Houghton Mifflin Company
Boston   1991

For Rachel

Library of Congress Cataloging-in-Publication Data

Zemke, Deborah.
    The shadow of Matilda Hunt / Deborah Zemke.
        p.   cm.
    Summary: Trouble follows Matilda Hunt like a shadow until she
figures out a way to get rid of it.
    ISBN 0-395-55334-2
    [1. Behavior—Fiction.] I. Title.
PZ7.Z423Sh   1991   90-46140
[E]—dc20   CIP
                         AC

Printed in the United States of America

WOZ 10 9 8 7 6 5 4 3 2 1

Trouble followed Matilda Hunt like a shadow.

On the way to the bus stop, Trouble
made Matilda jump in puddles and
throw her homework into the air.

In school, Trouble tickled Matilda
at the exact moment Mrs. Fretter was
saying something really important.

Trouble pinched Patrick Martelli and
made him cry.

"I didn't do it," Matilda told Mrs. Fretter.

But that just made matters worse.
Matilda had to stay inside for recess
and write "I will not lie anymore"
one hundred times.

Trouble just smiled.

Sunday was Matilda's mother's birthday. Matilda got up very early to make her a birthday cake. It was going to be an angel food cake with pink roses. But Trouble dropped a few eggs and a little flour and then ate all of the batter.

Trouble grew and grew until Matilda felt sick to her stomach.

"Boy, are you going to get it when Mom wakes up," said Matilda's brother Charles.

"I didn't do it," Matilda told Charles.

But Matilda had to stay home with Ralph
the babysitter while everyone else
went out for birthday dinner.

Trouble just smiled.

Matilda knew that she had to get rid
of her shadow. But how?

She got a shovel from the garage
and dug a big hole where the
ground was nice and soft.
She was going to bury Trouble.

"Wait until your dad sees this," said Ralph.

Trouble just smiled.

Then Matilda borrowed a few
stamps from Charles's collection.
She was going to send Trouble
someplace very far away.

"Wait until your brother sees this," said Ralph.

Trouble just smiled.

The zoo! They could keep Trouble with the other wild animals.

Matilda chased Trouble around the house. Around and around they went.

"That was your mother's favorite vase," said Ralph.

Trouble just smiled.

Matilda didn't know what to do. She
couldn't bury Trouble or send Trouble
far away. She couldn't even catch Trouble
with a butterfly net. Matilda stared out
the window at the moon.

The moon! She could send Trouble to the
moon. Matilda even knew where to find
a rocket ship.

She tiptoed out of her room, down the hall, through the kitchen, and out the back door. Trouble followed like a silent shadow. They crossed the back yard in the moonlight.

The rocket ship was sitting beside the garage. Matilda opened the lid and looked in.

"It looks like you're going to have to stay here while I go to the moon," Matilda whispered. "There's only room for one of us."

Trouble just smiled — and jumped in. That was exactly what Matilda wanted. She quickly slammed down the lid.

"Five, four, three, two, one . . . lift-off!" Matilda watched the rocket ship race toward the moon. She smiled as it got farther and farther away.

Matilda was happy. It didn't bother her when her mother said, "No TV for the next six weeks."

And it didn't matter when her father said, "You have to weed this garden for the next six Saturdays."

And so what if Charles said, "You have to clean my room for the next six years."

Matilda was still happy. Trouble was gone.

Matilda went inside and looked at the moon.
The moon just smiled.